GREAT ESCAPES
TERROR IN THE TOWER OF LONDON

GREAT ESCAPES

TERROR IN THE TOWER OF LONDON

BY **W. N. BROWN**

EDITED BY **MICHAEL TEITELBAUM**

HARPER

An Imprint of HarperCollinsPublishers

ISBN 978-0-06-286048-4 (trade bdg.)

ISBN 978-0-06-286047-7 (pbk.)

Typography by David Curtis and Laura Mock

21 22 23 24 25   PC/BRR   10 9 8 7 6 5 4 3 2 1

❖

First Edition

Lord Nithsdale's Escape from the Tower of London

Chapter One

UNDER SIEGE

Preston, England—13th of November, 1715

William Maxwell, 5th Earl and Lord of Nithsdale, clutched his musket with sweaty hands and gazed at the battle before him. All around, Scottish rebels were being ripped apart by British artillery, their blood spilling on the cobblestone street.

The tall, bearded Maxwell, or Lord Nithsdale as he was better known, crouched behind a wooden barrel as musket and cannonballs flew through the sky overhead. Black smoke from burning houses clogged the air and reddened every man's eyes, making it difficult to see.

The kilted Scottish Highlanders—Nithsdale's comrades from the mountains—were fighting to keep a hold over Preston, the northern British town they had invaded just four days earlier. Unfortunately, they were greatly outnumbered by red-coated British soldiers. They'd set up barricades to keep the British from entering the city, but holding them became increasingly difficult as the redcoats swarmed the town like fire ants.

Cold sweat ran down Nithsdale's bearded face, and his thumping heart felt as if it was going to beat out of his chest. He peeked around the wooden barrel and saw another Scotsman fall, killed by British musket fire as they tried to hold the makeshift barricade.

What are you doing? Nithsdale scolded himself silently. *You're the commanding officer in charge of that barricade! Get up and fight!*

And yet he stayed hunkered down. He thought of his wife, Winifred, and his son, both safe back home in Scotland, and wanted nothing more than to be back with them at their castle.

Why did I ever agree to go to battle? I'm no soldier!

Something zoomed through the air close by. Nithsdale jerked back as a cannonball crashed down on the street a few feet away, showering him with piercing shards of cobblestone fragments. The heavy iron ball bounced and then tore through a crowd of oncoming Scots like they were nothing more than sheets of paper.

The men's screams almost drowned out the gunfire. One of the Highlanders lay only a few feet away from Nithsdale, writhing in agony.

If you're not going to fight, you must at least try to help that man! Nithsdale thought. He closed his eyes, said a quick prayer, then hunched down and scrambled over to the fallen Scotsman.

The man lay in a pool of blood, his red eyes looking skyward, his teeth clenched. The cannonball had taken his arm off.

"Easy, lad," Nithsdale said.

He dropped his musket and, with some effort, managed to a scoop the screaming Highlander up over his shoulder. The two lumbered down the street and out of the line of fire, the Highlander cursing with every step.

By the time Nithsdale handed him off at the hospital tent, the Highlander was deathly pale. Nithsdale watched as others tried to stop the bleeding.

Poor devil. He ran into battle as I cowered behind a barrel, and yet he's the one who pays the price.

"Nithsdale!" His friend Lord Kenmure approached. "The British have us surrounded. There's no escape! We should have fled with the others when we still could."

Nithsdale didn't want to admit it, but perhaps Kenmure was right. The previous night, dozens of the Scottish rebels managed to silently slip out of town. A few of them had tried to convince Lord Nithsdale to join them.

"To stay is suicide," one said. "It will only end with your head on the chopping block."

Nithsdale had considered it. Though born in northern England, he had deep Scottish roots. On his twenty-first birthday, he had sworn his allegiance to the exiled Scottish king James—the same king the rebels were fighting to put back on the throne.

Feeling bound by honor and duty, Nithsdale chose to stay in the besieged town.

As he looked upon the dying Highlander, he couldn't help but regret that decision.

That night, Nithsdale and the rest of the leaders of the Jacobite forces met in a house. Jacobites were those who were fighting to get a Scottish king back on the throne. As the others talked about what to do, Lord Nithsdale peered out the window. Flames from the burning town licked the night sky. Beyond, camped on the hills just outside the city walls, was a sea of British tents with no end in sight. They clearly aimed to crush this rebellion now before the Scots made it farther south.

There must be at least three thousand redcoats out there, he thought. When the Jacobites had arrived in Preston, they numbered four thousand. Now they were less than half that.

"The British have the advantage," Nithsdale's friend Lord Derwentwater said. "It's over. We must surrender!"

"Aye!" Lord Kenmure said.

"Nithsdale," Thomas Forster, the general of the Jacobite forces, said from across the room. "What say you? Are you for surrendering, or shall we fight it out?"

Lord Nithsdale turned toward his fellow Jacobite noblemen. He ran a hand through his black hair and took a deep breath.

"The British have the town surrounded," he said. "And we're heavily outnumbered. I see no other option but to surrender and throw ourselves at the mercy of King George."

"Never!" barked a gruff voice.

The Jacobite noblemen looked over to a corner of the room where several Highlanders were gathered. Up until now, they had been silent. Old Brigadier Mackintosh of Borlum, leader of this group of Highlanders, stood up. "You noblemen may do as you wish, but there'll be no surrender from us. Our men can crush these British, and to surrender in an effort to save one's own skin would not only be foolish but an act of cowardice. We'll have no part in it." He let the words sink in. "Good night, gentlemen."

The Highlanders turned and walked out of the room.

No one said a word for a good minute. Nithsdale and the others waited on their general to speak first.

"Farmers," Forster finally said with a sneer, speaking dismissively of the Highlanders. "Those cattlemen are obviously ignorant of the reality of our predicament."

But they are brave, Nithsdale thought. *They fought while I hid behind a barrel.*

"I agree with Nithsdale and Derwentwater," Forster said. "To stay and fight is suicide."

At seven o'clock the next morning, Forster sent word to the British general that they wished to surrender. The British agreed, but only if the Highlanders would lay down their arms as well. Forster convinced a disgusted Brigadier Mackintosh, and soon the Jacobites were laying their swords and muskets down before the British forces in the town square.

THE JACOBITE UPRISINGS

From 1689 to 1746, a series of wars were waged between England and Scotland over who should be king.

Both countries shared a single ruler, but otherwise they were very different states—especially in terms of religion. Most Englishmen practiced a form of Christianity called Protestantism, while most of Scotland was Roman Catholic.

In 1688, when Nithsdale was twelve years old, James II was the king. James was born in Scotland and practiced Roman Catholicism. But the British Parliament was Protestant, so they wanted to dethrone James. Parliament started a war called the Glorious Revolution, in which they asked James's daughter, Mary II, and her husband, William III of Orange, to be joint monarchs. The effort succeeded, and a new Protestant queen was crowned.

Naturally, Scotland thought that wasn't fair, so over the next fifty-plus years, the Jacobites and their sympathizers—like Nithsdale—fought to put the rightful Scottish heir back on the throne.

They were called *Jacobites* because Jacob is Latin for James, the deposed king for whom they were fighting.

The war ended in 1746, when the Battle of Culloden proved to be the final Jacobite uprising, which the Jacobites lost. Prince Charles, the Scottish heir who organized the failed revolt, ran off to France. He tried to get support for another revolt attempt while in Europe, but couldn't find any takers.

Chapter Two

THE GATES OF HELL

London, Mid-December–10:22 p.m.

Lord Nithsdale felt nauseated as the stagecoach careened down the cobblestone street. He and the two other lords, Kenmure and Derwentwater, sat in silence as they bumped up and down in their seats. What was there to say? The three men were being taken to the dreaded Tower of London, where they would be held until they were sentenced.

Nithsdale shifted his arms in an attempt to alleviate the pain in his wrists, which had been rubbed red and raw from the heavy iron shackles placed around them. He'd worn them often, having spent the past few weeks being moved to different jails around England.

Glancing through the barred windows, he caught a glimpse of the stone archway they were headed toward. Nithsdale recognized it from afar as the famous Temple Bar gate. Then something else caught his eye, something he'd never seen on his previous visits to London—there were strange sticks lined up along the top the arch like porcupine quills.

Wait . . . what's on top of those poles?

When they neared the archway, he understood. There were severed heads stuck on the spiked tips. Some of the heads had their eyes open, staring blankly into the mist.

It feels as if I'm looking upon the Gates of Hell.

Nithsdale tried not to throw up as the carriage rolled through the gate. He thought about his wife, Winifred, and his son having to see his father's head on a spike and felt even more sick to his stomach.

After a few minutes, Nithsdale could smell the stink of the River Thames. He peered again through the barred windows of the stagecoach. Through the mist, he could see the foreboding stone wall of the Tower.

Armed guards kept a lookout from the top of

the wall. Beyond it, Nithsdale could see the four spires of the Tower stretching high into the night, lights flickering in their windows. There was a cluster of other buildings around the main tower, making the entire compound seem like a small city within the city. Nithsdale had never been to the Tower on his previous trips into London—he'd seen it only from afar, in the daytime—but he knew it was to be feared. "The Bloody Tower," he'd heard it called. Men and women held there were brutally tortured within its chambers and, more often than not, barbarically executed.

As a lord rather than a commoner, Nithsdale knew he would be granted a stay in one of the better cells and would not be tortured. It didn't really matter, though. Noble or not, he would be dead soon just the same.

Inside the Tower walls, he saw prisoners—most of them Scottish Highlanders—shivering in the cold as they were led off to their cells, shuffling past a blood-stained chopping block. One prisoner was manacled to a post where he was being brutally whipped.

"Halt!" came a loud, booming command.

The carriage stopped and the door opened.

"Out, all of you," the Tower Captain said, not looking up from the document he was holding.

Their hands in chains, the three noblemen stepped out of the coach and into the torch-lit courtyard.

"Those won't be necessary," the captain said, gesturing to the chains. "I doubt these traitors have any ill-conceived plans to fight their way out of here."

That was true. Nithsdale was no fighter. That's why he'd wound up here, after all.

The guard removed the rough iron manacles from Nithsdale's raw, bleeding wrists.

"You'll be held in the Lieutenant's Lodgings in the coming days and nights," the captain began. "Certain privileges will be granted to you, but my wardens will nevertheless keep you under watch at all hours, right up until you are sentenced. If any attempt to escape is made, you'll be tortured, along with any conspirators who aid said attempt. Are we clear, gentlemen?"

Nithsdale and the others nodded.

The captain led the new prisoners down a stone

walkway that wove around a large courtyard. Patches of grass peeked out from under the snow. To the left was the outer wall, where men armed with muskets kept watch in the torchlight. To the right stood the eighty-nine-foot-tall, four-spired main Tower. Nithsdale could see many of the captured Highlanders being led into the bowels of the building as guards barked orders at them.

Those men will never see the light of day again, Nithsdale thought. *Perhaps if we'd listened to them and tried to fight through the British defenses, things might've been different.*

He and his captors arrived at a cluster of buildings that made up the corner of the great outer wall. The three-story structures looked from the outside like any other wood and brick houses one might see in a nice part of London, except these were built into the wall of the Tower.

"Welcome to the Lieutenant's Lodgings," the captain said as the group arrived at the corner house. "This shall be your home for the near future."

"Though if it were up to us," one of the guards spat, "your traitorous hides would be in the darkest hole we could find."

The men walked through the door, stepping into a large common room. Servants came in and out, chatting with guards and one another while doing laundry or washing dishes. There were also a few children running around, which surprised Nithsdale.

He was separated from the other two prisoners and ushered through the room and up a winding stone stairwell. Atop the stairs was a small space large enough for a few men to gather. Two chairs sat on either side of a wooden door with a small, barred window.

The captain opened the door. "Your new home, milord. Enjoy your stay."

The door slammed and locked behind him. Nithsdale found himself in a small room, furnished solely with a bed, a small table, a chair, and a tiny bathroom consisting of a stone bench with a hole in it, into which he was meant to relieve himself. The contents would then flow into the toxic moat surrounding the tower. A barred glass window overlooked the stony ground between the inner and outer walls, sixty feet below.

This was where he would stay for the next

two months, with nothing to entertain him but thoughts of his sentencing, and the fact that he might soon be put to death.

God help me . . . I've never felt so alone.

Chapter Three

A PERILOUS JOURNEY

Somewhere in the English Countryside—8th of January, 1716

Winifred Maxwell pulled the wool scarf tighter around her face with a gloved hand.

She had never ridden on horseback in such harsh weather before. The howling wind brought gusts of snow right into her face, and the blowing flakes felt like knives on her skin. She clutched the reins with one hand, shaking, partly from the cold but mostly from fear that her husband was dead.

Please be alive, William, she thought, her teeth chattering. *If I get to London to find that you've been executed, I'll . . .* She couldn't even finish the sentence.

Only a few days earlier, Winifred had been sitting before a roaring fireplace in her drawing room at Terregles Castle in Scotland. She was sewing a quilt and trying to relax. With her husband away fighting the English, she had been on edge the past few weeks. Spending the holiday with her young son had brought a welcome distraction, but that had soon faded.

The silence had been interrupted by a loud knock at the front door, causing the needle to slip and prick her finger. Winifred cursed silently before calling for her handmaiden Cecilia to answer. It was a messenger, and he carried a letter.

Hastily, Winifred tore open the letter and began reading.

"It's from William!" she cried. "He's alive!"

At first, she was relieved to hear Lord Nithsdale had been captured and not killed in battle. She knew her husband well, and he was no soldier.

But then the letter said, *I am to be sentenced soon, I know not when. I'm being held in the Tower.*

And any sense of relief she'd had crumpled to pieces.

"What shall we do, milady?" Cecilia asked.

"We go to London, of course! Perhaps there's something I can do to save him from the executioner's blade."

"In this storm?" Cecilia protested. "How? The closest stagecoach is more than a hundred miles away."

"We have no choice, Cecilia," Winifred said. "I must see my husband before it's too late. Start packing and have the servants get the horses ready. We'll have the maid look after little William while we're gone."

That was two days and eighty-six miles ago, and now they had just crossed the Scottish border into England. Winifred's and Cecilia's horses were up to their knees in the snow, going as fast as they could, but Winifred feared it wasn't fast enough.

As she rode, memories pulsed through her mind of the last time she'd nearly lost a loved one to the Tower. Winifred's father, the 1st Marquess of Powis and a devoted Catholic, had been falsely accused of trying to assassinate King Charles II in 1678, shortly before Winifred was born. He was imprisoned in the Tower for a few years, during which time Winifred's mother was almost arrested for plotting to free him. He was released when Winifred was a young girl, but the memories had always haunted him.

Even though he was a noble, Father was tortured within an inch of his life, she thought. *He could never move his arms the same after they were stretched on the rack.*

If they were giving her husband the same treatment, she would not be able to bear it.

THE STORY OF GUY FAWKES

Winifred's husband and father were only two of the Tower's many famous captives. Another was one of England's most famous would-be assassins, Guy Fawkes. Though he was imprisoned a century before Nithsdale, both fought the House of Stuart to restore a Catholic king to the throne. The country was in religious turmoil when the Protestant

James I, the first Stuart king, took the throne in 1603. The monarchy wanted to institute an entirely Protestant system to diminish the power of the Catholic Church in government. This meant a lot of Catholics in England were treated unfairly. Many were fined, imprisoned, or even executed.

Fed up, a small group of Catholics decided to take matters into their own hands. Their plan: blow up the Houses of Parliament building with the king and anti-Catholic lords inside. Their means: thirty-six barrels of gunpowder, which they'd hidden beneath the House.

Apparently one of the plotters got cold feet and sent an anonymous letter to the authorities, saying that Parliament "shall receive a terrible blow." The king had the Houses of Parliament searched. Sure enough, the gunpowder was found, along with former soldier and conspirator Guy Fawkes, who said he was guarding the barrels. Fawkes was arrested and taken to the Tower of London.

Fawkes was questioned in the very same room where Lord Nithsdale would stay a hundred years later. Unwilling to reveal the identities of his coconspirators, he was arrested, taken into the White Tower, and tortured. By one account, he was hung from the ceiling by his manacled hands, confined in the tiny "Little Ease" room, and stretched on the rack for two and a half hours.

He eventually gave up the names of five of his coconspirators before being returned to the Little Ease room. The king sentenced him to be hanged and quartered, the most brutal punishment carried out at the time. It entailed dragging a man on a wooden panel by horse, then hanging him almost to the point of death. From there, the criminal was mutilated, beheaded, and chopped up into four pieces, which were then put on display around England. After the noose was put around his neck, Fawkes managed to jump from the platform, breaking his neck. This saved him from an agonizingly painful death.

Fawkes came to be the figurehead of the Gunpowder Plot and a symbol for resistance to persecution. His capture and the discovery of the gunpowder

are celebrated every November 5 in England on what's called Bonfire Night. Today, Fawkes is perhaps best known for the masks made from his likeness, which were featured in Alan Moore's graphic novel *V for Vendetta* and worn by members of the hacker group Anonymous.

Suddenly, Winifred's horse faltered in the deep snow, losing its footing.

"Whoa!" she yelled, grabbing the saddle horn.

She almost fell off, but the animal recovered. They were only a few miles from Newcastle, where they could take the stagecoach the rest of the way to London. The sun had gone down and night was falling. Up ahead, Cecilia's horse stopped in its tracks.

"What is it?" Winifred called out, yelling to be heard over the howling wind.

Cecilia motioned for her to be quiet. She pointed into the woods. Several pairs of glowing red eyes bounced around between the trees in the darkness.

The hair on the back of Winifred's neck rose.

Wolves! Winifred thought. She was face-to-face

with four of them. The growling beasts were creeping slowly toward the women's whinnying horses, their fangs bared in the light of the full moon.

Winifred gritted her teeth and removed a pistol from her cloak. There was no time for second thoughts. She fired a shot into the air, and prayed.

At the sound, the wolves spooked and ran off into the woods. Winifred let out a long, shaky breath.

"Let's pick up the pace!" she shouted, kicking her horse. Winifred couldn't help but feel that the wolves had been some kind of bad omen. She needed to get out of these woods, and to her husband, now.

Chapter Four

DEATH SENTENCE

London, England—19th of January, 1716

"Out of the carriage!" the guard barked.

Nithsdale and the two other arrested Jacobite lords climbed out of the stagecoach and stepped onto the damp London street. Before them stood Westminster Hall, the lights from its hundreds of windows shining in the night.

I have friends in Parliament, he reassured himself. *Surely they can convince their comrades to spare a fellow Englishman's life.*

The guards ushered Nithsdale and his fellow prisoners through the massive doors of Westminster Hall. The courtroom was cavernous, almost like a cathedral. Lining the stone walls were

scores of men seated in bleachers. At the back, in the center of the room, sat the Lord Speaker. He was gray-bearded and had a white wig atop his head. This was the man from whom the defendants would hear their fate.

Though he'd been hopeful before, Nithsdale realized how wrong he was upon walking into court. Cold sweat beaded his brow as he found himself before the sea of unfamiliar powdered faces, sneering in disgust at the sight of these traitors to the crown.

These men despise the Jacobites, Nithsdale thought, *and even more so a Jacobite sympathizer like me . . . God help me, I'm doomed!*

"You three men stand before the court accused of treason," the speaker bellowed, his voice echoing throughout the chamber. "How do you plead, Lord Kenmure?"

The powdered faces in the cavernous Westminster Hall courtroom smirked as Lord Nithsdale peered up at them from the marble floor. The few faces he did recognize certainly didn't look sympathetic.

"I plead guilty," Lord Kenmure said. "Though I submit that I had no prior knowledge, when I chose to join the Jacobites on their ride, that I would be going to battle with Britain."

The courtroom scoffed loudly.

Perhaps we should have come up with a better excuse, Nithsdale thought.

Lord Derwentwater went next, repeating the sentiments of Kenmure.

Desperate to see his family again, Nithsdale decided to take it one step further. As disgusted as he was with himself for his conduct in battle, he knew that if ever there was a time to beg for his life, it was now.

"I plead guilty, Your Honor. But like Lords Kenmure and Derwentwater, I too had no prior knowledge that I would be going to war when I agreed to ride out with my fellow countrymen. I beg for your pardon and your mercy. I do not wish to leave my son fatherless, nor to leave my wife a widow."

The chancellor sneered.

"You should have thought of your wife and

31

whelp before you foolishly decided to take up arms against King George," he growled. "The question is whether or not you three men, Lords Kenmure, Derwentwater, and Nithsdale, are guilty of treason. As many as are of that opinion, say 'Aye.'"

Nithsdale's jaw clenched when the white-powdered faces erupted, their "Ayes" echoing throughout the chamber.

The speaker nodded. "And of the contrary, 'Nay'?"

A deafening silence now filled the room.

"The 'ayes' have it," the speaker said. "It is this court's verdict that you three men are guilty of the crime for which you are accused. You will be taken to Tower Hill, where your head shall be removed from your body. Guards, take this traitorous rabble back to the Tower."

20th of January, 1716–4:15 p.m.

"Ugh," Cecilia gasped, holding her scarf to her nose as they finally rode into London. "That's quite an odor."

Their horses were practically limping after the grueling four-hundred-mile journey. They'd arrived in Newcastle over a week ago to find that the stagecoach had been canceled, leaving Winifred and Cecilia with two options: wait for the snow to melt so the roads could clear, or make the rest of the trip on horseback. They chose the latter.

Now, after almost two weeks of riding, Winifred's nose rankled at the smell of the city. It was so different from the clean air of the Scottish countryside. Horse waste was everywhere, and raw sewage covered the cobblestone streets. Rats, feral cats, and street urchins ran in and out of garbage piled high in the snow banks. The dark gray sky coupled with the constant misting rain made it all the more depressing.

BAD PLACE TO VISIT, WORSE PLACE TO LIVE

London in the early eighteenth century (the 1700s) was filthy and overcrowded. The city's destitute lived in cramped, dirty buildings, often with a family sharing a single room. Many resided in government-built "workhouses" where people could do jobs like sewing in exchange for food and living space.

The death rate among children was high due to malnutrition, with seventy-four percent dying by the age of five. Orphaned or abandoned children ran wild in the streets.

The city would only get more crowded as the century continued. In fact, the population of all of Britain grew rapidly, from around five million people in 1700 to nearly nine million by 1801. This was due to the Industrial Revolution, which began in the eighteenth century and caused even more people to move to the city for jobs in factories.

After riding through the city's countless slums, Winifred and Cecilia reached the more wealthy Covent Garden area. The two women rode slowly through the horse and wagon–filled streets. Winifred noticed some red-coated government officers talking near one of the taverns.

"Stay here," she said to Cecilia. "I'm going to see if I can get some information from those policemen." She climbed off her horse and stepped down onto the damp street. After Cecilia had taken hold of the horses' reins, Winifred approached the British officials.

"I beg your pardon," she said. "But could one of you gentlemen be kind enough to tell me if the noblemen Jacobite sympathizers have been sentenced yet?"

"Absolutely, ma'am," one of the soldiers told her. "Heard they were sentenced just last night, as a matter of fact. I believe the traitors are to face the executioner's blade on the twenty-fourth of February."

He's alive! My husband is still alive!

Winifred resisted the urge to jump in the street, only allowing herself a small smile.

She now had five weeks to work out a plan to rescue him.

That evening, Winifred paid a visit to the Tower of London. She peered up at the forbidding stone structure. From the ground, the four spires of the Tower loomed in the dark sky like the horns of a giant monster. Flickering lights emanated from the windows as if they were the creature's eyes. She felt chilled to the bone to think of her husband there, inside the belly of the beast.

Now I know how my mother felt when she paid my father a visit all those years ago, she thought.

She squared her shoulders, marched across the bridge, and introduced herself to one of the guards.

"I am the Countess of Nithsdale," she said, "and I am here to see my husband, Lord Nithsdale."

The guards looked at one another.

"The only way a wife of the condemned is allowed to see 'er husband," one of them said, "is if she's confined with him in the Tower until his sentence be carried out. I'm sorry, rules are rules—countess or no."

"I'm afraid confinement would be quite detrimental to me in my poor health," Winifred lied. "Might I please see him?"

"My condolences for ye' 'illness,' madame," one of them replied, obviously not buying her story, "but the answer's still no."

"Look," she said, removing a few coins from her

pocket. "I've ridden an awful long way and am very tired. My lord is to be executed in a month, and I'd like to see him. Have some food and drink tonight on me, and my gratitude."

The guards looked at each other again and grinned.

"Right this way, milady," one of them said, taking the money and leading her inside.

Winifred shuddered at a scream she heard upon entering the courtyard.

"That's probably not your husband," the guard said. Then he smirked and added, "But I can't be certain."

TORTURE AT THE TOWER

There were at least forty-eight prisoners tortured at the Tower of London during the sixteenth and seventeenth centuries, and those were only the ones that were documented.

Three brutal torture methods were used at the Bloody Tower:

The rack: Perhaps the most famous, the rack

was a wooden device with rollers on both ends. Prisoners were tied to it by their arms and legs, and when a wheel was turned, the ropes would pull the two halves of their body in opposite directions.

The manacles: Prisoners were forced to stand up on wicker steps, lift their arms, and place their hands through two iron gauntlets called manacles attached to a steel bar. The prisoners were left to hang by their wrists, their legs dangling as the steel manacles ground into their skin and bone. It is believed that Guy Fawkes was tortured this way.

The scavenger's daughter: Prisoners were put in an iron device that kept them kneeling down. It could be tightened with a screw. The scavenger's daughter worked in the reverse way of the rack—by compressing the person, as opposed to pulling them apart—and was extremely painful.

There was one more method of torture used at the Tower, called the Little Ease. It was a tiny, windowless room measuring nearly four square feet, not big enough to sit, stand, or lie down in. Prisoners were forced to crouch in the dark space in greater and greater agony until they were let out. Though not as brutal sounding as the others, it was still excruciating. Eventually the tiny room was sealed up. It is said to be located somewhere in the White Tower dungeon.

The guard led Winifred east, toward the Lieutenant's Lodgings, the group of half-wooden town houses next to a small, grassy area, with trees arching overhead.

"This section doesn't seem as frightening," Winifred mused. Maybe her husband was not suffering as much as she'd feared. "It's quite peaceful, really. . . ."

The guard chuckled and pointed. "Be even more peaceful once we clean the blood stains."

Winifred gasped. Beneath one of the trees was a large stone block, and she saw now it was covered

in large red stains, as was the cobblestone floor surrounding it.

"Spot's quite famous," the guard continued. "That's where the Countess Margaret Pole was executed. Over a hundred years ago, it was. The executioner was inexperienced. She lays her head on the block, he hits her once on the neck with the ax, and then she stands up and starts running around screaming! Blood squirting all over the place, they say! Poor lady had to be restrained, and it took ten more whacks to finish the job." The guard shook his head. "I pray your husband's executioner has a more sure hand, for his sake. . . ."

Aghast, Winifred did her best to force a smile. "Yes, one can only hope."

He wants you to be afraid, she told herself. *Don't you dare give him the satisfaction.*

They entered one of the buildings, the front of which looked like a timbered, three-story cottage. After passing through a large antechamber where some officials were talking, Winifred was led through a small passageway and ascended a winding series of stone steps. At the top were two guards seated at a table next to a locked door with a small barred window. Playing cards and gambling chips were strewn about on the table.

I'm nearly there, Winifred thought, shaky with anticipation, joy, or fear—she couldn't tell which. It had been so many months and hundreds of miles since she'd last seen her husband, and now he was only inches away, on the other side of that door.

One of the guards, tall and skinny, got to his feet. He leaned over and nudged his short, bearded friend awake.

"What we got here?" he said in a strong Cockney accent. "A visitor, eh?"

"It's Lord Nithsdale's wife," said the guard who had been accompanying her. "Come to see her husband. Lady Nithsdale, this is Otto and Elmer."

"How do you do," Winifred said, shaking their hands and slipping them some coins. *I need to get them on my side,* she thought. *Make them believe that we're friends. Whatever it costs.* "Please have a token of appreciation for letting me see my husband."

Then Winifred glanced up through the small,

barred window and felt her heart stop.

There he was. Her husband. His beard had grown longer, and his face seemed more weathered, but otherwise he was the same man she'd fallen in love with so many years ago.

Otto noticed Nithsdale as well and snapped at him, "Stand back from the door. You've got a visitor. Whoops, clumsy me . . ."

Winifred bit her lower lip in annoyance as the guard slowly bent down to pick up the keys he'd dropped. He then spent precious seconds fumbling with the key in the lock. *I will grab those keys out of your incompetent hands and open that door myself,* she thought, balling her hands into fists.

At last, at last, the door opened and she tearfully ran into her husband's arms.

"Oh, my dear husband!" she cried.

They held each other for a long moment. He was alive. They were together. For now, that was enough.

She pulled back to look around the room and was relieved to see that her husband's nobleman status had at least gotten him nicer quarters than some of the other prisoners. The chamber was small, but it had a table, chair, and bed.

After the guards closed the door behind them, Nithsdale spoke, his voice raw with emotion. "Thank God you're here, Winnie. I've missed you and little William terribly. It's all I can think about in this place. I hope your travels here weren't too difficult."

Winifred laughed and wiped away her tears. She recalled the wolves, the snow, the canceled stagecoach. "It was a little chilly" was all she said. "Now, let me look at you. Still handsome as ever, I see. I was terrified you'd been wounded in battle, or worse."

Nithsdale frowned and nodded. He turned away from her and walked to the small desk at the foot of his bed.

"I'm afraid that you have shown more courage simply by coming here than I did in battle." He pounded his fist on the wood. "Fight gallantly, I did not. Instead, I ran. I have disgraced our name with my cowardice."

"You have not disgraced anyone! I'm just glad you're alive."

Nithsdale gave a weak smile and touched his wife's cheek.

"Here's the truth of it," he said. "I'm not ready to die. I didn't want to die in battle, and I don't want to die by execution. I want fresh air, the countryside, time with you and our son, as much as I can squeeze out of this life."

"I want that as well," said Winifred, holding his hand in hers.

"There are those who are willing to martyr themselves for our true king, the Scottish king," he went on. "I met many of these brave men in battle. They would gladly die to help the cause, or to prove our point. I am not one of them." He looked at her and said simply, "I am afraid, Winnie."

Winifred swallowed hard. She was afraid, too.

"There must be a way out of this," she tried to reassure him. She peered out the barred window of his cell and found herself looking three stories down upon a stony street.

"I can't exactly jump out the window," he said, following her gaze.

"Tomorrow," said Winifred, "I shall go to visit

the king and plead for leniency. If I can hand him a petition for your release, I'm sure he will grant it."

Nithsdale looked skeptical. "I'm here because I fought to overthrow the king. I don't expect him to look favorably upon me."

"Traditionally, the king of England will never refuse a request from a desperate lady," Winifred said. "Especially one of means."

"Yes, but may I remind you that this king is originally from Germany—he has different values than the English. Furthermore, how will you get an audience with him—you, the wife of a condemned Jacobite?"

I have absolutely no idea. "I will work it out," she promised. "We will get your freedom, and then we'll be together once more. We'll leave Britain, go someplace safe, where we're not the enemy."

She went to hold her husband once more when there was a tap at the door. The guard Otto was back. "Time for the lady to depart," he ordered.

Lord Nithsdale kissed his wife's hand. "To think," he said quietly, "this is one of our last nights together."

"It won't be," she assured him. *It can't be.* "I will find a way. And until I do, I will be back here every day to see you. Be strong, my love. You are not alone."

He gave her a small, sad smile. "As long as you're by my side, I could never be truly alone."

It was difficult, but she finally turned and walked out of the cell, tears clouding her vision.

After following Otto down the stairs, Winifred took notice of all the activity in the council room: officers conferring, servants cleaning, children playing.

"My word!" she said. "Is it usually so busy?"

"Most times, yes, ma'am," Otto said.

It's a very social house, Winifred thought. And with that, a plan began to form in her head.

Chapter Five

BEGGING THE KING

21st of January, 1716

The next morning, Winifred took a stagecoach to St. James's Palace, the king's towering residence in central London. Knowing full well that there was no way King George would grant her an audience, Winifred realized that she was going to have to sneak into the palace.

She and Cecilia were staying with Mrs. Mills, a Jacobite sympathizer and friend, who lived in a luxurious Drury Street town house. Mrs. Mills, who was also six months pregnant, had lent Winifred the maidservant's outfit that she was wearing now, hoping to enter the palace unnoticed.

When Winifred had told her friends of her plan

the day before, Cecilia had grown worried.

"But those caught sneaking into the palace could be imprisoned," she had argued. "Or even executed!"

"They wouldn't dare execute the wife of a nobleman."

Yet now that Winifred was at the palace, she had her doubts. What if she was wrong?

You've come this far, Winifred. No turning back now. You must do it for William! She disembarked from the stagecoach, straightened her dress, and approached the servant's entrance.

Armed royal guards stood flanking the entrance. But Winifred wasn't intimidated by the government officials, having grown up around them all of her life as the daughter of an English nobleman. With a bag of cleaning supplies in hand, she walked right up to a young and foolish-looking officer.

"Terribly sorry to disturb you, me lord," she said in her best Cockney accent. "But I'm here to do some dustin' in the chapel and the queen's chamber."

"No one told me about more servants arriving at this hour," the guard said.

Oh no! Winifred thought. *The maids must have already visited today. Quick, Winnie, think fast. . . .*

"Oh, well, I guess the queen's room'll be a bit dusty tonight," Winifred replied. "I'll be shoving off, then."

The guard gritted his teeth. Winifred held her breath and tried to look meek and dull, just an ordinary woman with a job to do.

"Fine," said the guard. "Proceed."

"Bless ye, sir."

After walking through the cavernous passageway, she found herself in a vast stone courtyard. Compared to Whitehall—the palace where the royals had stayed before it burned in a fire eighteen years earlier—St. James's Palace was relatively small. Winifred hoped it wouldn't take long for her to find the king. With each passing moment, it became more likely that someone would catch her.

I've got to move fast!

Entering through the east wing, she walked through the rooms at a quick pace, stopping to dust only when guards or other servants passed by. After moving through numerous doorways and dusting countless vases and statues, she finally found herself in a chamber with His Majesty, King George.

Winifred removed a petition for a sentence appeal from her cleaning bag and approached the monarch. The king, wearing a large, lavish robe that spread out all over the polished wood floor, paid her no mind. And why would he? She was just a maid, after all.

This is my one chance to save my husband, Winifred thought. *I have to make it count!*

A rush of emotion came over her, and she threw herself at the king's jeweled slippers. Winifred knew George's grasp on the English language was weak. Her German wasn't that great either, so she pleaded with him in a language they both knew—French.

WHY DID ENGLAND HAVE A GERMAN KING?

It may seem strange to think that a non-English-speaking German could become the king of England. As mentioned in the previous sidebar, Great Britain was in religious and political turmoil for most of the seventeenth century (the 1600s), which led to the Glorious Revolution to dethrone the Catholic king James II. Parliament wanted a Protestant sitting on the throne, not a Catholic, because a Protestant king could be made to share power. A Catholic monarch, however, would claim he or she was only answerable to God or the pope.

The next few kings and queens were Protestant or Anglican, and when a Catholic was next in line for the throne in 1701, Parliament put through the Act of Settlement, which simply bypassed the Catholic and went directly to the next Protestant successor. After Anne, queen of Britain, died in 1714, she was to be succeeded by her nearest Protestant relative of the Stuart line. This was Sophia, daughter of Elizabeth of Bohemia, James

I's only daughter. But Sophia died a few weeks before Anne, and so the throne went to Anne's second cousin, the fifty-four-year-old George Louis from Hanover, Germany.

To Parliament, it didn't matter that King George I was from Germany—they just cared that he was a Protestant.

"Your Majesty," Winifred sobbed in French. "I am the unfortunate Countess of Nithsdale, wife of Lord Nithsdale, and I've come to plead for my husband's life. Forgive the ruse, but I had to disguise myself as a maid to gain audience with you. I beg you to spare my lord's life, Your Majesty. Please, I beg you, show him mercy, please. . . ."

The king looked down into Winifred's teary eyes, and his rubbery lips curled into a sneer.

"GUARDS!" he called in German before attempting to walk out of the room.

Any fear Winifred had left her as she grabbed the tails of George's great robe. Undaunted, the king pressed on, and Winifred slid across the floor, desperately clinging to the fabric.

"Please, Your Majesty . . . Please!"

He made it out of the room and into the hall-way, still dragging Winifred with him. Then two guards were upon her, shouting and prying her from the king's robe.

Tears streaming down her face, Lady Niths-dale dropped the petition as the one man with the power to save her husband's life walked away from her. He did not look back.

Chapter Six

LADY NITHSDALE'S PLOT

12th of February, 1716

With the date of her husband's execution now less than two weeks away, Winifred was growing increasingly desperate. Thankfully, the king had not imprisoned her for sneaking into the palace, but neither had he given any response to her petition. As Nithsdale had predicted, the king would not save him. Yet that did not stop his wife from passing the petition on to their mutual friend, the Duke of St. Albans, who had given Lady Nithsdale his word that he would present it to the House of Lords.

"I cannot lie to you, milady," the duke told her. "In the end, I believe my efforts shall do little to save your lordship's head."

"I know," she replied. "But you must try."

She had visited her husband in his cell every day. Nithsdale said he was resigned to his death. But Winifred was not one to quit, and she had one more scheme up her sleeve.

"My lady, you must be joking," Cecilia whispered upon hearing Winifred's next plan. The two were in the drawing room of the Millses' house, where they'd been staying since their arrival in London. "Walk right out of the Tower with your husband, in plain sight of the guards?"

"That's right," Winifred replied.

"And how do you plan to do that?"

Winifred glanced around to make sure no servants were in earshot. Then she whispered her plan in Cecilia's ear. Cecilia's eyes widened.

"Wouldn't the guards notice a six-foot, bearded figure walking out of a cell?"

"Not if the disguise was done right," Winifred said. "The men who work there have grown to like me over the last few weeks, and I think their goodwill may afford me some leeway in bringing in and out other visitors."

Maybe that wasn't entirely true. But they certainly did like the coins she gave them every time she visited.

Winifred knew Cecilia well, and she could see that her trusted assistant wasn't so sure about this new scheme. Cecilia's doubt didn't make Winifred feel any more confident. "I know this plan seems ridiculous," she continued, "but it may be the only thing that will save my husband from the chopping block!"

"Then we must try it," Cecilia said. "What can I do to help?"

Winifred paused. She looked at Cecilia in the candlelight, so bright-eyed and faithful. Was she taking advantage of her handmaiden? Anyone who helped her would be risking at best imprisonment, and at worst their life. But she had to ask—the plan needed multiple people to work.

"Endangering your life isn't one of your duties," Winifred said. "If we are caught in our scheme, we could become imprisoned in the Tower as well. And there's a good chance that we'd face the executioner's ax, just as my lord does."

"Of course I'll aid you, milady," Cecilia said without hesitation. "Tell me what needs to be done."

"We must find identical cloaks, dresses, caps, and skirts—four or five of them at least. Also, if you have a trusted friend—a tall friend—that lives in town, see if you can rope her into our plot. The more women we can find who are as tall as my husband, the better. And remember, it must be someone you can trust with our lives."

Cecilia nodded seriously. Winifred felt a pang of maternal love for this girl, who had worked with the Nithsdale family for many years. *At least if she is caught,* Winifred thought, *we will be punished together.*

"And remember," Winifred added. "It may not come to this. I am still hoping the petition I gave the duke will pass."

She wasn't able to put much hope in her voice, though. She didn't think the Duke of St. Albans would be able to convince the king to free her husband.

If the king would refuse the begging wife of a

nobleman, she thought, *what chance would the duke have?*

"Why the good mood, milady?" Elmer asked. "Have never seen youse so happy 'afore."

Winifred smiled as she handed the guard a pound. "We're celebrating. A petition passed tonight that might very well save my husband's life!"

Elmer grinned, his mossy brown teeth illuminated in the candlelight. Otto, whom Winifred had just seen talking to a handmaiden in the nearby council room, joined them.

"I won't believe he's walking out of here till I sees it meself," he said, sitting down next to Elmer and picking up his hand of cards that he'd left on the small table. "Sorry, milady."

Winifred kept the smile plastered on her face and handed the surly guard a pound. "Well, go out and celebrate anyway. Might I see my husband so I can give him the good news?"

However, when Otto closed the cell door behind him, Winifred's smile faded.

"Listen," she said to her husband in a low voice. "A petition to parole some of the prisoners has indeed gone through, but your name was not among them."

Nithsdale's face fell. "But . . . I heard you out there, with the guards . . . you told them there was good news."

Winifred looked back at the door, making sure no one was by the window. "I didn't want to tip them off. You see, I am going to get you out of here without a petition. Tomorrow night, I shall slip you right out the front door."

Nithsdale's stunned disbelief grew as Winifred revealed to him the scheme to dress him up like a lady.

"Are you mad?" he gasped once she had finished explaining. "This plan will never work! You'll be caught and executed alongside me, and then our son will be orphaned!"

"Keep your voice down," she hissed. "I tell you, it will work! It must work! Now listen, you'll have to shave your beard and—"

"Perhaps I can attempt to climb out the window," Nithsdale interrupted. "The bars seem as if they can be loosened. I could fashion a rope with some bedsheets and—"

Winifred's dry laughter cut him off. "Those bars aren't going anywhere," she said. "And even if you did manage to wrench one free and somehow climb the three stories down, the guards would see you."

And a rope of tied-together sheets, Winifred thought, looking at her large husband, *wouldn't be enough to hold you!*

FALL OF A PRINCE

Winifred was right—escaping out of a high window was a bad idea. One man who tried, and failed, was Welsh prince Gruffydd ap Llywelyn. In 1244, the prince had been imprisoned in the Tower of London for three years. His cell was located ninety feet up in the White Tower, which was one of the four towers of the Inner Ward.

Determined to escape, Gruffydd made a rope from sheets and cloth. On March 1, he climbed out of the window. Unfortunately, the rope he'd made wasn't strong enough to hold his weight and poor Gruffydd fell to his death. The guards would later discover a grisly sight: the impact had shoved his head clean into his chest.

"I'll have no part in it!" Nithsdale blustered. "I'd rather die before going through with such a humiliating charade!"

Winifred narrowed her eyes at her stubborn husband. "William," she said clearly, calmly. "In four days, you are due to be put to death with all of London watching, leaving me a heartbroken widow. I have considered every option, tried every approach. This is our only hope. If you are going to let your fear of humiliation stand in the way of your freedom, then you are not the man I thought you were."

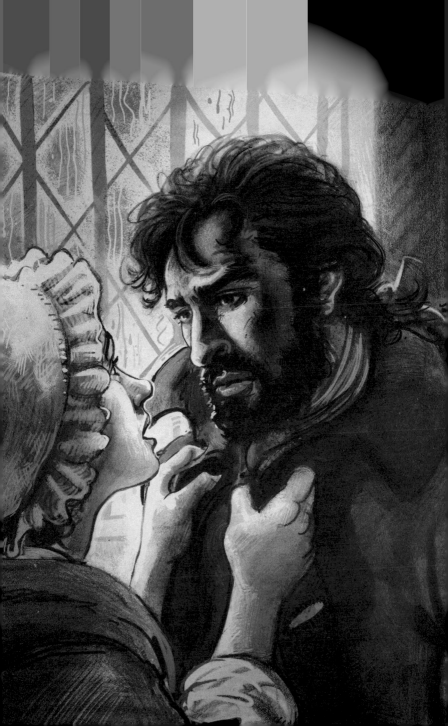

Chapter Seven

EVE OF EXECUTION

23rd of February, 1716

Lady Nithsdale's heart was racing when she descended the stairs of Mrs. Mills's home for the final time. It would soon enough be dusk—the time when she had told the coachmen to pick her up. In less than twenty-four hours, her husband was scheduled to be executed. She could feel the time slipping away from her.

Winifred had gotten very little sleep the night before, between worrying and working to get everything ready. If she'd forgotten anything, she told herself, she'd simply have to improvise. This was little comfort, however, as one mistake could ruin everything, and now Nithsdale's life wasn't the only one depending upon their success.

Mrs. Mills was sitting in the drawing room, having tea with Cecilia, and Cecilia's tall friend Miss Hilton, who had recently moved to London from Scotland.

Winifred walked up to her host. "Mrs. Mills," she said, "you have been so kind to us, allowing us to stay with you for these past few weeks. I now have one more big favor to ask of you. As you know, tomorrow my husband is to be executed. I am leaving for the Tower now, as are Cecilia and Miss Hilton. We are going to help him escape. I need your aid, but know that in doing so you would be risking imprisonment. I wouldn't dare ask if my husband's situation were not so dire."

Mrs. Mills looked surprised. "What is your plan?" she asked

"We are going to visit my husband's cell," Winifred told her. "We'll all dress in the same hooded cloaks. Miss Hilton will be wearing two of them, and shall give my husband one to put on. We'll make a big fuss, weeping and wailing, going in and out of his cell. This should hopefully create enough confusion to allow his lordship to slip out in disguise. The guards, I pray, will simply think he's one of the grieving women and not keep a close count on the number of people who leave. You and Miss Hilton are as tall as my husband, and as you are pregnant, your belly is as large as his. The guards will be less likely to question a tall, large-stomached woman leaving the cell if they see at least one entering it."

Winifred took a breath. Silence hung in the air as she let her friend think it over. With her height and pregnancy, Mrs. Mills was absolutely crucial to the plan.

"You have a baby now to think about," Winifred continued. "If you don't want to do this, of course I'll understand. I wouldn't dare—"

"I wish to help," Mrs. Mills finally said.

Winifred smiled and hugged her friend.

"You have just saved my husband's life. I'm glad that you agreed, because otherwise the red wig we bought would have been a waste."

Mrs. Mills was taken aback. "You have a red

woman's wig for my lord to wear?"

"Of course," Winifred said. "It had to match your hair!"

Snow had been falling all day. What little sun managed to peek through the grayness was just beginning to set over the River Thames as the stagecoach left Mrs. Mills's house on Drury Street. Winifred gave each of the women identical oversized brown cloaks to wear.

"Remember, you must put on two cloaks," she told Miss Hilton, as you are the slimmest, and therefore the one least likely to be noticed for wearing two. One is for you, the other for my husband. Likewise, Cecilia is wearing two dresses under her cloak."

Miss Hilton nodded. "I thought one of them looked too big for her," she said.

Winifred kept rambling about the plan, even though there was nothing new left to say. She didn't want to give the other ladies too much time to think. It wasn't a long coach ride—only ten minutes or so—but that was more than enough time for one of the women to change her mind about taking part. Even though Winifred assured them that she herself would be the only identifiable one and that the others would use handkerchiefs and cloak hoods to cover their faces, it was little guarantee that they wouldn't fail.

"I can hardly believe I'm doing this," Mrs. Mills said, her hands resting on her pregnant belly as the coach bumped along the cobblestone street. "How exciting! 'Tis a good thing my husband is out of town; he'd want me having no part in it."

Winifred faked a smile. *Dear God,* she thought. *If we are caught, may no harm come to my friends.*

Darkness was beginning to fall over London as the coach pulled to a stop in front of the Tower. Cecilia and Miss Hilton climbed out and stood for a minute, gawking at the foreboding stone walls and four spires. Winifred saw the fear flash in their eyes—the reality of what they were about to do was setting in.

"It will be all right, ladies," she assured them. *I hope. . . .*

She told the driver to wait outside the walls, then hurried the women toward the entrance. The guards recognized Lady Nithsdale and let the four of them enter the courtyard. Mounds of snow covered the stone walkways and grass. There was a narrow, fresh-trodden path through the snow for the women to walk to the Lieutenant's Lodgings.

Winifred knocked on the door. The three women behind her were already playing their parts, crying and sniffling. The hoods of their cloaks were pulled over their heads, and they held handkerchiefs to their faces. Winifred was impressed with her friends' acting performances.

"Ah, Lady Nithsdale," Otto said after opening the door. Behind him, guards and handmaidens were talking and walking around the antechamber, as usual. "I was sorry to hear your husband was not among the prisoners being paroled. Terrible news indeed."

"Thank you, Otto," she said. "Might I see my husband in his hour of need?"

"Aye, you may. I'm afraid your friends will

have to stay here, though."

Winifred's heart skipped a beat. How would her plan work if the other women couldn't enter the cell?

Chapter Eight

LORD NITHSDALE'S DISGUISE

23rd of February, 1716–9:17 p.m.

Winifred's mind raced. She had to tell the guard something to persuade him to let them all into the cell, and she had to do it fast!

"Please, Otto," she asked. "My friends were very close with my lord, he was like family to them. I beg of you—they'll be very quick, they just want to bid him farewell before he's executed tomorrow."

Otto rolled his eyes and sighed.

"Please . . ." Winifred asked again, feeling real tears spring to her eyes.

"Oh, very well. But you may take only one of them at a time."

This would make the plan more difficult, as she

wouldn't be able to hide her husband in a crowd of women. But this was as far as Otto would budge.

She thanked the guard profusely before turning to Miss Hilton and waving her onward. "Well, you heard the man—let's get on with it! Come on, come on. . . ."

Crying dramatically, Miss Hilton hurried into the antechamber. Winifred nodded a sad hello to the small crowd as she led her friend through along by the arm. At the opposite end of the room, the two entered a small hallway and ascended the stone steps to Lord Nithsdale's cell.

At the top of the stairs, next to the cell door holding some playing cards, sat Elmer. "I heard the sad news, ma'am," he said. "I'm sorry." And indeed, he sounded genuine.

"Thank you, dear Elmer," Winifred said. She moved aside for Otto, who took a chair next to his partner. "There's still a chance another petition will go through tomorrow and grant my husband a reprieve."

Elmer forced a weak, brown-toothed smile. "At least he's got a good wife like you to comfort 'im in these dark times."

He stood and opened the cell door. Winifred and the loudly grieving Miss Hilton shuffled inside. Once the door was shut behind them, Winifred ran over to her wide-eyed husband.

He's shaved his beard, she noticed. *Excellent!*

"We're really doing this?" he murmured.

Rather than reply, Winifred began speaking loudly about the new petition for his release that would hopefully go through tomorrow. As Miss Hilton sobbed, she removed one of the cloaks she was wearing and handed it to Lord Nithsdale.

"Hang on to that," Winifred whispered.

"But what about this other petition you speak of?" Nithsdale whispered back.

"It's a lie—there is no petition. Now you just sit down and let me put this makeup on you."

Nithsdale didn't have to be told twice. Winifred continued speaking loudly about the petition as she removed a small bag of makeup and began applying it to his cheeks and around his eyes.

"Enough crying, now!" she said to Miss Hilton. "Go out and fetch Mrs. Catherine, so that she may

bid my lord goodbye."

Miss Hilton walked out of the cell. A minute later, a weeping Cecilia arrived.

Lord Nithsdale smiled when he saw the familiar face. Cecilia grinned back, but kept up her grieving act. She removed her cloak and the additional, extra-large outer dress she wore and gave it to Nithsdale to put on. She then walked out, nodding to Elmer and Otto, who hardly looked up from their card game.

"My dear Mrs. Catherine," Lord Nithsdale called out after her, "pray go in all haste and send in my wife's chambermaid!"

He looked down at his wife and smiled.

"You're quite the actor," Winifred said.

The "chambermaid" Mrs. Mills came walking up the stairs next, holding the handkerchief to her face and bawling. As the tall, pregnant woman lumbered in, Winifred was putting the final touches of makeup onto her husband. She whitened his dark eyebrows and face stubble.

Having finished with the makeup, Winifred brushed his black hair back and placed the curly red wig on his head, one that looked similar to Mrs. Mill's fiery locks. With the wig secured, she pulled the hood over it while making sure some of the curly red hairs stuck out. Then she had him get to his feet.

Standing next to each other—hoods on, lower faces covered—Lord Nithsdale and Mrs. Mills could pass for twins.

This actually might work, Winifred thought.

Lady Nithsdale nodded to her husband, who immediately held the handkerchief to his mouth and hunched over.

Winifred closed her eyes and steeled her nerves.

Leaving a brave Mrs. Mills in the cell, Winifred led Lord Nithsdale, now crying loudly into the handkerchief in his best Mrs. Mills impression, through the door.

Please let Otto and Elmer be suitably distracted by their card game, she thought.

They'd only gone a few steps out of the cell when Elmer laid a hand on Lord Nithsdale's cloaked shoulder. Winifred's lungs seemed to stop working, and her heart felt like it would explode.

We've been caught. It's over.

"There, there, milady," Elmer said, consoling his disguised prisoner. "It'll be all right, it will."

Lord Nithsdale, his head down, nodded his thanks and continued his grieving act. Winifred tried to smile at the guard.

"You're so kind. She'll be fine."

Elmer shook his head grimly.

"The way she's going on," he said, "you'd think it was her being executed tomorrow."

Winifred laughed nervously. Then she led her husband down the stairs and into the crowded antechamber. Everyone seemed too wrapped up in their own conversations to pay any attention to the two weeping women walking through—after all, this was the Tower of London, and here they were used to mourning.

Winifred and her husband were almost to the door when a loud "Wait!" stopped them in their tracks. Winifred turned to see Otto running down the stairs.

Winifred tried not to panic. She kept her face as still as she could but was gripped by the sense that Otto could see right into her mind. *Should we run for it? We'll never make it!*

Otto wasn't smiling. He looked at her, then at the weeping "woman" by her side. Winifred watched the guard stare at her hunched-over husband for what could've been five seconds or five minutes—time seemed to stop. Then he walked past them and opened the door.

"I was so caught up in cards I'm afraid I forgot me manners," he said. "After you."

Winifred exhaled. "She's very upset," she said. "Thank you, Otto."

Lord Nithsdale shuffled through the door and into the company of Cecilia. She would be taking him to the stagecoach, where Miss Hilton was already waiting.

Back inside, Winifred turned to Otto.

"I'll go bid my husband farewell now," she said. *We're not in the clear just yet. . . .*

She returned to her husband's cell, where Mrs. Mills was anxiously waiting. After Elmer had shut the door behind her, she approached her friend.

"Wait a few moments," Winifred said. "I'll let

you know when the time is right."

She began speaking loudly in a deep voice in an effort to imitate her husband's. Then she answered in her own. Mrs. Mills looked at her as if she was crazy. Still, she had to buy a little time.

After a few minutes had passed, she gave her brave friend the nod. Mrs. Mills began sniffling again and exited the cell.

She made it down the steps successfully and was halfway to the exit, when Otto grabbed her by the shoulder, stopping her in her tracks.

Mrs. Mills held her breath as the guard removed her hood. He wore a mystified look as he stared at her face, looked at the door, then back at her face again.

"Yes?" she asked.

"Sorry, milady," he said. "Lost track of who was comin' and goin', there be so many of ye'."

"No trouble at all," Mrs. Mills said.

Her heart resumed beating as she walked out the door and headed for the stagecoach.

Back in the cell, the minutes ticked by as Winifred loudly discussed with herself petitions, hope, and prayers. Finally, enough time had passed for her husband to get to the nearby safe house. She opened the cell door and shut it hard behind her.

"Please don't disturb my husband, Elmer," she told the half-sleeping guard stationed by the door. "He's deep in prayer."

Elmer nodded and told her not to worry.

Winifred walked down the stairs and into the antechamber, telling anyone who would listen to please leave her husband in peace. Most assured her they would or gave her a dismissive nod. On the way out, she ran into Otto once again.

"Good night, ma'am," he said. "I promise not to disturb his lordship. And God be with ye'."

She thanked him one last time, and walked out into the snow.

Winifred's carriage stopped in front of a town house just north of the Tower, overlooking a small cluster of buildings and courtyards called Tower Hill. Winifred's adrenaline was still pumping when she stepped out and walked to the front door. Her hands were shaking and she couldn't stop smiling. She'd beaten the Tower! She wished her parents were here to see this.

They would be proud of me, she thought, remembering her father's stories about the horrors he'd experienced at the Tower. She felt like she'd gotten revenge tonight for him as well. Then she caught herself. *Don't celebrate now . . . You're not out of England yet.*

As long as they were in this country, both their lives would be in danger. And before she could leave Britain, there was one last thing she needed to do.

One thing at a time, she cautioned herself. She knocked on the front door. A female friend of Mrs. Mills opened it.

The older woman waved Winifred in and quickly shut the door behind her. She took Winifred up the stairs and then up a small ladder to the attic. Nithsdale was sitting on a small cot in the cramped space, speaking with Cecilia in the candlelight. His face lit up when he saw Winifred climb into the room.

"I can't believe you did it," he said, embracing

her. "You saved my life. I've always known you were a resourceful woman, but I am in awe of you."

"We're not out of the woods quite yet," Winifred cautioned him. "By the time the sun rises, they'll be looking for us."

Chapter Nine

A GRISLY SIGHT

24th of February, 1716—9:40 a.m.

Winifred embraced Mrs. Mills in the drawing room of the safe house.

"You shouldn't be here," Winifred told her. "It's too dangerous."

"I had to stop in to tell you the news. I just spoke with the Duchess of Buccleuch. Apparently, her husband was present when the king was told of your escape. Word has it he flew into rage unlike anything the court had ever seen!"

Lady Nithsdale winced, yet she couldn't help but smile.

He should've granted my petition when he had the chance, the swine!

"His face was flushed red, and spittle was flying everywhere," Mrs. Mills continued. "He ordered that all military in the area are to find the both of you at once. He now wants both your heads for this humiliation!"

The smile on Winifred's face vanished.

"You took a great risk in coming here," she said. "And you should go. But I owe you a debt that I can never repay."

She hugged her brave friend once more.

"Thank you."

An hour later, Lord and Lady Nithsdale stood by the attic window, watching the large crowd in the snowy street on Tower Hill. Angry peasants were screaming for blood as Nithsdale's two friends who had been captured alongside him at Preston marched up the icy steps onto the wooden platform.

Lord Kenmure was first. He said a few words, but Winifred couldn't hear them—he was drowned out by the crowd. He then kneeled and bravely laid his head on the wooden block.

The hooded executioner stepped up. He raised the ax above his head, then brought it swiftly down. It struck with a dull thud. The crowd cheered.

"I can't bear to look," Winifred said, turning away from the window.

Lord Nithsdale kept his eyes on the execution. "I feel that I don't deserve to look away," he remarked quietly. "I escaped while they did not. The least I can do is watch them as they go."

After the guards removed the head and body of Kenmure, Lord Derwentwater stepped up to the block. Before he kneeled, he said a few words. "My only regret is pleading guilty. I pledge my allegiance to the Roman Catholic Church and King James. Long live the king of Scots!"

The bloodthirsty mob cheered even more this time as the ax came down, then erupted when one of the guards held the head up for onlookers in the back to see. Lord Derwentwater's mouth was somehow still moving.

OUCH! WHAT IT REALLY FEELS LIKE TO LOSE YOUR HEAD

Thankfully, beheading is a thing of the past in most parts of the world, but historians remain fascinated with the subject. Thanks to modern science, we now know what such a gruesome fate would feel like. First, if your head is on the chopping block, you'd better hope you have a skilled executioner with a sharp, heavy ax—separating a head from a body is no easy feat. Will it hurt? Even with the above components in place, definitely for a split second (no pun intended) or two.

It has also been documented that heads can blink for a few seconds after being lopped off. During the French Revolution, people were guillotined by the thousands, and some heads were seen blinking after being chopped off. In 1977, when a man was beheaded in France for the last time, the head was reportedly responsive for thirty seconds. Today, doctors believe that blinking or mouths moving post–head loss are simply the nerves and reflexes twitching. They also believe that consciousness is lost about two to three seconds after you lose your head.

Nithsdale swallowed hard and looked at the floor. "My poor friends." He turned to Winifred. "That would have been me down there if it weren't for you."

Winifred bit her lip. *It could still be you, Husband, or me. . . .*

"We're not safe yet," Winifred said. "Every soldier in London is looking for us. Mrs. Mills says she has a friend in the Venetian embassy who can smuggle you out of the country. A carriage to take you from here has been arranged."

Nithsdale looked out the window again. Officials were dragging his friends' headless bodies to a cart, leaving a trail of blood in the snow.

"At the moment, Italy sounds very agreeable," he said. "Can this friend smuggle you out as well?"

This was where Winifred had to tell him the truth, that their fantasy of being together in a safe land couldn't come true—not now.

"I can't leave yet." She took a deep breath. "I'm

afraid I must return to Scotland."

Nithsdale looked at his wife as if she were crazy. "You're a wanted criminal! If they catch you, you'll be executed! No, you can't. I forbid it! We'll simply arrange for someone to take our son to meet us in Italy."

"The message could be intercepted," Winifred argued. "I shudder at the thought of the British holding our child hostage in exchange for our surrender. Besides, I have the family titles hidden on the property and only I know the location. I must return. It's the only way."

"I'll go with you," he said.

"No. They'll be looking for us to travel together. We'd be caught."

Nithsdale swallowed hard. He accepted that his wife had made up her mind and that there was no changing it. She was going back to Scotland.

"I feel like I've found you, only to lose you again," he said.

The look he gave Winifred broke her heart, but she remained steadfast.

"You'll never lose me," she said. "I promise."

◆◆◆

The next night, a coach arrived to take Lord Nithsdale to the Venetian embassy. Before he entered the carriage, Nithsdale embraced his wife for what he feared could be the last time.

"If you're arrested," he told her, "I'll return and offer myself in your place."

"Don't worry about me," she said. "I'll be joining you in Italy soon enough."

Nithsdale shook his head. "You know, you are the brave one. You always have been." He kissed her. "Goodbye, my love."

After the carriage had left with her husband, Winifred put on her cloak and met Cecilia, who was just down the street with the horses. Winifred climbed into the saddle and looked up.

"A moonless night," she said. She quickly checked her pocket to make sure she had her pistol. "Luck is with us."

"Let's hope so," Cecilia replied.

Chapter Ten

LORD AND LADY FUGITIVES

The English Countryside–5th of March, 1716

Winifred bolted upright in the icy grass, pistol at the ready. Though bleary eyed in the mid-morning sun, she could see it was only Cecilia approaching.

"Don't shoot!" her maid said. "I brought some food from the nearby town."

They were in the middle of the woods. Now that Winifred was a wanted criminal, the women had to keep to the fields, forests, and hills, as King George's men would be patrolling the main roads. They'd been riding through the night and sleeping throughout the day. What was already a long journey from London to Scotland was now even more unbearable.

"You'll scarcely believe it," Cecilia said, handing

Winifred a piece of cooked meat. "There are Wanted posters up all over town and on the roads, with etchings of you and my lord's faces. There's a hefty reward for aid in your arrest."

"I believe it," Winifred said before biting into the meat. The leg of lamb shook in her gloved hand. Though she was heavily bundled up and it was daylight, she was still freezing. As desperately as she wanted to build a fire, she knew it could attract the attention of King George's men.

She was cold and hungry, sore from riding, and terrified of being caught. To make matters worse, she couldn't stop imagining her husband getting stopped on his way out of the country. He could already have been found out. He could be dead, and she'd have no way of knowing.

I just need him to make it to Italy, she prayed, as though thinking could will it into being. *We're almost safe.*

London–7th of March, 1716

Lord Nithsdale grunted and pulled at the collar of the tight Venetian clothing. The servant's uniform given to him by Mrs. Mills's friend in the Venetian embassy was a size too small and the wig he wore hot and uncomfortable, but he didn't care. Up ahead were the docks, and the boat that would take him to freedom.

Easy, Maxwell, he thought to himself. *You don't have much farther. . . . Keep your calm. . . .*

He tried to keep his eyes down and look inconspicuous as he walked among the other Venetian servants, but it was difficult. Nithsdale towered above the other men trailing the Venetian ambassador's carriage as it rolled down the London street.

The disguised Lord's eyes darted back and forth, scanning the crowd for any British officials.

I know I'm going to get recognized, he thought. *Whether it's by a redcoat or a civilian . . . There are Wanted posters with my face all over the city! How could they not see through this disguise?*

The Venetian caravan suddenly came to a halt. There was a commotion up ahead as other carriages moved to the side of the road.

What's going on?

Then Nithsdale saw it—the king's carriage was

passing through! Nithsdale looked at the ground, sweat dripping down from under his wig.

"One side for the royal carriage!" screamed some officials.

After a few seconds, Nithsdale couldn't resist. He looked up just in time to see the carriage passing by. And sitting right next to the window was the king himself, George I!

For a brief moment, Nithsdale locked eyes with His Royal Highness.

My God . . . does he recognize me?

Time seemed to freeze. Could he really have come all this way, only to wind up right back where he started?

I'm so sorry, Winnie, he thought. *I've failed us both.*

And then George yawned and looked away.

The royal carriage moved on, and the Venetian caravan, with Nithsdale among them, continued to the docks.

That was all.

May that be the last time I ever set eyes on the king, Nithsdale prayed.

Finally, the Venetians and Lord Nithsdale boarded their ship. As they set to sea, Nithsdale stood on the deck and looked back at his homeland, straining to keep it in his sights for as long as possible. He knew that he could never return.

He would start a new life in Italy. He just hoped that his wife and son would be there with him.

Scotland–11th of March, 1716

Winifred dashed through the hallways of Terregles Castle. Only a few weeks before, she had left this place the well-regarded wife of a nobleman. Now she returned a wanted criminal. The lieutenant of the county, a friend, had assured her he would warn her if he heard of any British coming for her. This did little to comfort her.

She'd arrived at Terregles two days earlier. Having arranged for the family's valuables to be taken and stored at a friend's property in nearby Traquair, she only had one more piece of business to attend to.

She walked up a set of stairs, stopping at a

portrait of her father hanging against the wall. After removing the painting, she opened a secret compartment and removed a tin box. Inside, the family titles were dried out but otherwise in good shape. The papers ensured that the Nithsdales would keep the family land and fortune despite their crimes against the throne.

"Thanks for watching these for me, Father," she said, before rehanging the portrait.

She then walked out of the front door and into the chilled air.

"Find them all right?" Cecilia called from her horse. In front of her on the saddle sat little William, Winifred's five-year-old son.

Winifred nodded. She looked up at the place she'd called home for so long. It was where she and her husband had raised her son—a property that had been in her family for over half a century. She knew this was the last time she'd see it.

"Mother, what were you doing in there?" her son asked.

Winifred snapped out of it.

"Just retrieving some things I didn't want to

forget, honey," she said. "Are you ready to take a trip to see your father?"

The little boy nodded enthusiastically.

"Thankfully this ride will be a bit easier," Winifred told Cecilia as she got on her horse. Unlike their first journey to London, there was no blizzard to trek through.

"It's not the ride I'm worried about," Cecilia replied, clutching the young boy with one hand and the reins with the other. "I'm more nervous about returning to London, where everyone's looking for you."

"It's the only way we can get to Italy," Winifred reminded her. If there were a ship that left from Scotland, instead, of course she would take that in a heartbeat. But there wasn't. Her only route to freedom was through the city where she was most in danger.

London—14th of March, 1716

It was night by the time Winifred's stagecoach pulled up to the Port of London on the River Thames.

Known as the busiest port in the world, the place was a congested mass of humanity. People from all walks of life, from rich socialites to homeless orphans to foreign sailors, squeezed by one another, each one focused on their own destination.

Winifred paid the driver as Cecilia grabbed their two bags. Winifred took young William by the hand as they navigated the teeming crowd. She kept a hood over her head to help cover her face, staring at the ground whenever a British official passed by. And there were a lot of them.

"There it is!" Cecilia said, pointing to a ship about fifty yards off. "Dock 52."

The three were almost there when Winifred stopped in her tracks, the hair standing on the back of her neck. Government officers were checking passengers' identifications before they boarded. And one of them had the Wanted poster with drawings of Lord and Lady Nithsdale in his hand!

"Relax," Cecilia told her. "This is why we got falsified identification papers made."

Winifred squeezed her son's hand and tried to be calm. Her heart was beating a mile a minute. *I'm so close!* she thought.

"If I'm caught," she said to Cecilia in a low voice, "please take care of little William."

The three-minute wait to board felt like three centuries. But then, when they reached the front of the line, it felt far too soon. She wasn't ready.

"Papers, miss?" the official requested.

Stay calm, Winnie. . . .

Winifred smiled nervously. She handed the falsified documents over. As the man looked at them, she couldn't tear her eyes away from the Wanted poster with her likeness in his hand.

The official handed the papers back, staring directly at her. As she took the documents, he grabbed her by the wrist, hard.

"Well, well," he said. "Winifred Maxwell."

Winifred dropped her papers and went pale. Cecilia grabbed little William.

"I've got her!" the man said to the other officer. "I found Lady Nithsdale!"

Now what? What do I do?

"What are you on about?" Winifred protested, trying to appear outraged. "You're mad!"

"Mad like a fox," the officer said. "The spittin' image, you are! I'll be getting a promotion for this."

People stopped what they were doing and stared. A crowd began to form. Panicked, Winifred looked over at Cecilia and her son. Little William began to cry.

Your son is scared, Winifred realized in her frantic state. The best thing, for his sake, would be to not make a scene and go quietly.

She hung her head and was just about to admit defeat, when a loud voice cut through the air.

"Spaulding! What are you doing?"

Another officer, older and in better dress, walked over. He looked at Winifred, then turned to her captor.

"I found her!" Spaulding said. "Lady Nithsdale!"

The superior officer turned once more toward Winifred. He stared coldly into her eyes. She thought he could see right through her, and struggled not to look away. Then he glanced up at her hair.

"Let her go, you blithering idiot," he told Spaulding. "Lady Nithsdale has wavy blond hair."

He reached up and took between two fingers one of the red curls sprouting out from under Winifred's hood.

WANTED FOR TREASON

LORD & LADY
NITHSDALE
JACOBITE TRAITORS

DEAD OR ALIVE

"This woman's hair is nothing like that. Are her documents valid?"

"Well," Spaulding sputtered. "Yes, but—but . . ."

"'But—but' nothin'!" his superior said, cutting him off. "Now unhand the lady and apologize!"

The official's face turned red. He looked down and retrieved the fallen documents, mumbling apologies all the while.

"Sorry, ma'am. You really do look like the lady we're after."

"Quite all right—everyone makes mistakes," Winifred said. "Perhaps I should be flattered. I hear Lady Nithsdale is a very beautiful woman."

She grabbed one of the bags Cecilia had dropped and followed her handmaiden and son onto the boat. She reached up and touched the red wig on her head. It had saved her husband, and now it had saved her, too.

An hour later, the ship pulled out. From the river, Winifred could see the fearsome Tower of London, its four spires standing against the full moon.

Goodbye, England, she thought. *And good riddance.*

EPILOGUE

Lady and Lord Nithsdale were happily reunited in Rome. Though they could never return to Scotland and had little money, the two were content just to be alive and well with their family. Lord Nithsdale passed away in 1744, at sixty-eight years old. Following his death, Winifred discovered he'd left them in debt. She lived another five years before dying at age sixty-nine.

The story of Lord Nithsdale's escape quickly became an international sensation, though in her later years, Winifred would humbly shrug it off. And though King George I once said of Winifred that she had done him "more mischief than any

woman in Christendom," he softened on the subject over time. He later said of Lord Nithsdale's
escape, "For a man in milord's situation, it was
the very best thing he could have done."

Today, tourists visiting the Tower of London
can see the very room where the escape took place.
The cloak Lord Nithsdale wore was recently on
display at a museum in Traquair, Scotland.

AUTHOR'S NOTE

In order to streamline the narrative, some dates had to be changed. Lady Nithsdale actually left for London on Christmas day, arriving shortly before her husband's sentencing. In the book, their reunion takes place after Lord Nithsdale is already sentenced so that Winifred could begin working on William's release sooner. Also, the son—William the Younger—was twelve or so and away in Europe at the time of the escape (though sources vary on this). This was changed to ratchet up the stakes for Winifred's escape from the country. Other liberties were taken with the story as well, such as the scene at the end with the wig and police. And finally, it is highly unlikely that Winifred ever ran into wolves in the woods of northern England, as the last known wolf in Great Britain had been killed somewhere in the Scottish Highlands thirty-five years before.

SELECTED BIBLIOGRAPHY

Bilyeau, Nancy. "The Tiny Cell called 'Little Ease' was the Most Feared Room in the Tower of London." *The Vintage News*, April 21, 2018. https://www.thevintagenews.com/2018/04/21/little-ease/.

Blundell, Frederick Odo. *Ancient Catholic Homes of Scotland*. London: Burns & Oates, 1907. http://www.kirkcudbright.co/historyarticle.asp?ID=380&p=17&g=4.

Bunting, Tony. "Battle of Preston." *Encyclopedia Britannica*. Encyclopedia Britannica, Inc., November 2, 2019. https://www.britannica.com/event/Battle-of-Preston-1715.

Freeman, Shanna. "Top Ten Myths about the Brain." HowStuffWorks.com, Sept. 17, 2008. https://science.howstuffworks.com/life/inside-the-mind/human-brain/10-brain-myths6.htm.

"George I." English Monarchs. http://www.englishmonarchs.co.uk/hanover.htm.

Jones, Nigel. *Tower: An Epic History of the Tower of London*. St. Martin's Press, 2012.

Lambert, Tim. "A Brief History of Poverty in Britain." http://www.localhistories.org/povhist.html.

Leisure, Susan. "The Extinct English Wolf." https://animals.mom.me/extinct-english-wolf-3154.html.

Maxwell, Winifred. *A Letter from the Countess of Nithsdale*. London: J. Rider, 1827.

McCallum, Robert. *The Jacobites*. http://www.instebook.com/JACOBITE.HTM.

Ridgeway, Claire. "The Execution of Margaret Pole, Countess of Salisbury." The Anne Boleyn Files, May 27, 2010. https://www.theanneboleynfiles.com/the-execution-of-margaret-pole-countess-of-salisbury/.

Thornbury, Walter. "Westminster Hall: Notable Events," in *Old and New London: Volume 3*, (London: Cassell, Petter & Galpin, 1878), 544-560. British History Online, http://www.british-history.ac.uk/old-new-london/vol3/pp544-560.

"Torture at the Tower." Historic Royal Palaces:
   Tower of London. https://www.hrp.org.uk/tower
   -of-london/whats-on/tower-torture/#gs.8zz61y.

White, Matthew. "Poverty in Georgian Britain." Oct.
   14, 2009. https://www.bl.uk/georgian-britain
   /articles/poverty-in-georgian-britain.

ABOUT THE AUTHOR

W. N. BROWN is a writer and journalist from Henderson, Texas. In addition to authoring *Great Escapes: Civil War Breakout* and *Great Escapes: Tower of Terror*, he has written countless articles on historical artifacts, scientific discoveries, and popular culture. He currently lives in New York City.

ABOUT THE EDITOR

MICHAEL TEITELBAUM has been a writer and editor of children's books for more than twenty-five years. He worked on staff as an editor at Golden Books, Grosset & Dunlop, and Macmillan. As a writer, Michael's fiction work includes *The Scary States of America*, fifty short stories, one from each state, all about the paranormal, published by Random House, and *The Very Hungry Zombie: A Parody*, done with artist extraordinaire Jon Apple, published by Skyhorse. His nonfiction work includes *Jackie Robinson: Champion for Equality*, published by Sterling; *The Baseball Hall of Fame*, a two-volume encyclopedia, published by Grolier; *Sports in America, 1980–89*, published by Chelsea House; and *Great Moments in Women's Sports* and *Great Inventions: Radio and Television*, both published by World Almanac Library. Michael lives with his wife, Sheleigah, and two talkative cats in the beautiful Catskill Mountains of upstate New York.

Turn the page for a sneak peek at the next
DEATH-DEFYING GREAT ESCAPE!

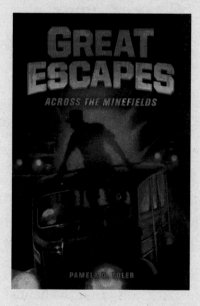

Chapter 1

THE SIEGE

Bir Hakeim, Libya, Africa—June 8, 1942

Susan Travers heard the whine of the approaching planes. She put on her helmet and kneeled on the floor of her dugout, waiting for the next German air raid to start.

Imagine you're in a deep underground bunker, she told herself. *Imagine your helmet is a huge metal umbrella that bombs bounce off, like hailstones from a roof.*

She knew in reality that the helmet would not protect her if a bomb hit, but it was better than nothing. She had lived in a tent at other military camps, but that would have been too dangerous in this Free French outpost in the Libyan Desert.

Her home here was a narrow trench dug into the sand. It was ten feet long, four feet wide, and waist deep—big enough to hold a camp bed, a little folding chair with an attached table, and her suitcase. The walls were reinforced with sandbags to keep them from collapsing, and a thin piece of sand-colored canvas stretched over the top to protect her from the sun during the day. But it wouldn't protect her from a bomb any more than her helmet would.

Right now, as she waited for another wave of the German dive bombers, called Stukas, to attack, she thought it looked more like a shallow grave than a refuge.

Susan could hear the Stukas now, droning in the distance like a vast swarm of bees headed toward Bir Hakeim. They were the worst part of the German attacks, in her opinion. As the sound grew nearer, she felt her heart pound and her legs tremble. It seemed like the bombers' humming was *inside* her head.

Abruptly, the sound changed into high-pitched screams, followed by silence as the planes dived toward earth and released their bombs. The silence was almost worse than any of the noises. Five long seconds of quiet as bombs fell toward their targets on the ground.

Susan counted the seconds in her head, the way she had when she was a little girl waiting for the lightning after a clap of thunder. *One, two, three, four, five—*

The shells hit the ground right on time, exploding with a blinding flash. The earth shuddered. Then debris and dust filled the air.

"Please let it be over," she whispered.

Susan knew the siege would have to end soon. General Koenig, the commander of the besieged French forces, had refused to surrender to German commander Erwin Rommel. This meant Rommel would have to come in after them. The French troops couldn't hold out much longer. Susan's garrison was running out of food, water, and ammunition. Soon they would have no choice but to give up.

When the war with Nazi Germany began three years earlier, Susan had eagerly volunteered to help her beloved France, first as a nurse and then as a driver. But she had never imagined that she would end up in Africa with the First Free French Brigade, fighting to keep the Germans out of Africa.

Susan and the Free French forces under the command of General Marie-Pierre Koenig had arrived at Bir Hakeim on February 14, 1942. After nearly four months in the desert, most of the soldiers wanted nothing more than to leave. But not this way. Not in defeat.

Their job was to help stop the German army from advancing into Egypt. The encampment at Bir Hakeim had been the least important and most remote Allied post but now, suddenly, it was the focus of Rommel's force—the Afrika Korps. Susan had come here expecting boredom, not action.

That changed in late May. Commander Rommel ordered the Afrika Korps to change direction and head straight for Bir Hakeim. For almost two weeks since, he had rained down artillery shells on the outpost and across the no man's land of barbed wire and anti-tank minefields that surrounded it. Air raids battered the French camp day and night. The fighting only stopped when a sandstorm rolled in from the desert, making it impossible to see either friend or foe.

The Germans had help as well. They had allied with the Italians, who had superior tanks. All around Susan and her fellow soldiers were dangerous minefields and beyond that, the German and Italian forces encircling the camp.

The desert was also their enemy. Bir Hakeim was an old fort on a sand-blown plateau, a flat area only slightly higher than the land around it. There was no shade, and sometimes, even now in June, the temperature reached as high as 120° Fahrenheit during the day. At night, when the sun went down, the temperature fell below freezing, and Susan shivered in her dugout, unable to sleep.

Now, when the dust from the air raid settled, Susan looked out of her dugout to see where the bombs had fallen. The mobile van that served as the general's headquarters was untouched. So was the officers' kitchen, which was only halfway underground.